I060050б

Rest

Samuel D. Hunter

SAMUEL
FRENCH
FOUNDED 1830

SAMUELFRENCH.COM
SAMUELFRENCH-LONDON.CO.UK

FOR PRODUCTION ENQUIRIES

UNITED STATES AND CANADA
Info@SamuelFrench.com
1-866-598-8449

UNITED KINGDOM AND EUROPE
Plays@SamuelFrench-London.co.uk
020-7255-4302

Each title is subject to availability from Samuel French, depending upon country of performance. Please be aware that *REST* may not be licensed by Samuel French in your territory. Professional and amateur producers should contact the nearest Samuel French office or licensing partner to verify availability.

MUSIC USE NOTE

IMPORTANT BILLING AND CREDIT REQUIREMENTS

Please Note:

REST was commissioned and first produced by South Coast Repertory

REST was developed at The Ojai Playwrights Conference; Robert Egan, Artistic Director/Producer

Initial developmental work on REST was done in the Clubbed Thumb Writer's Group; Maria Striar, Artistic Director

REST was first produced by South Coast Repertory in Costa Mesa, California on March 28, 2014. The performance was directed by Martin Benson, with sets by John Iacovelli, costumes by Angela Balogh Calin, lights by Donna Ruzika, original music and sound by Michael Roth, and dramaturgy by John M. Baker. The Stage Manager was Sue Karutz and the Assistant Stage Manager was Jamie A. Tucker. The cast was as follows:

ETTA	Lynn Milgrim
TOM	Hal Landon Jr.
GERALD	Richard Doyle
FAYE	Sue Cremin
GINNY	Libby West
JEREMY	Rob Nagle
KEN	Wyatt Fenner

REST was then produced by Victory Gardens Theater in Chicago, Illinois on September 12, 2014. The performance was directed by Joanie Schultz, with sets by Chelsea Warren, costumes by Janice Pytel, lights by Lee Keenan, and sound by Thomas Dixon. The Stage Manager was Tina M. Jach. The cast was as follows:

ETTA	Mary Ann Thebus
TOM	Ernest Perry Jr.
GERALD	William J. Norris
FAYE	Amanda Drinkall
GINNY	McKenzie Chinn
JEREMY	Steve Key
KEN	Matt Farabee

CHARACTERS

The residents:

ETTA – Early to mid-eighties, female.
TOM – Eighties, male.
GERALD – 91, male.

The staff:

FAYE – Late-thirties, female.
GINNY – Late-thirties, female.
JEREMY – Forties, male.
KEN – 20, male.

SETTING

The entrance area and common room of a small, white, dry-walled rest home in northern Idaho in January. One side of the stage is dominated by a large, automatic glass sliding door that makes just a bit too much noise whenever it opens. Through the door there is a foyer, and another unseen sliding glass door offstage. Near the glass door is a small reception desk with a dusty old computer on top, a telephone, a jar filled with hard candy, etc. A large window is on one side of the stage. Above the reception desk is a large dry-erase calendar with very few events or activities written in. An empty wheelchair or two might be appropriate. To the other side of the stage is a small common area with a couch, a recliner or two, some folding chairs, a coffee table, and a television.

The entire place has been mostly packed up, and labeled boxes are littered across the stage. The feel of the stage should be institutional, sterile, and contained.

NOTES

Dialogue written in *italics* is emphatic, deliberate; dialogue in ALL CAPS is impulsive, explosive. Dialogue written in *BOTH* is a combination of the two.

A "/" indicates an overlap in dialogue. Whenever a "/" appears, the following line of dialogue should begin.

Ellipses (...) indicate when a character is trailing off, dashes (–) indicate where a character is being cut off, either by another character or themselves.

ACT ONE

Scene One

(Afternoon, nearing dusk. **ETTA** *sits on a chair,* **KEN** *sits near her.)*

ETTA. The end of our adulthood, I suppose. We sort of unexpectedly (and expectedly I guess) slid back into infancy. Gerald in diapers, struggling to put names to faces, words to objects, meaning to –.

(short pause)

You really want me to talk about this?

KEN. Really. Please.

ETTA. I'm like a stereotype, telling you all this. Like some old woman stereotype, droning on about her life.

KEN. No, really, I –. Please.

(Pause. **ETTA** *looks at him.)*

ETTA. It's not a bad place to spend three days. Not a particularly good one either, but. The ambience is par for the course, maybe sub-par now that it's been dismantled a bit. The food is awful, but I'm hoping you can help us on that front. You're a good cook?

KEN. I guess?

ETTA. You have experience?

KEN. I mean, kinda? I worked at a Taco Bell in high school.

ETTA. Well that's not nothing, I guess.

(pause)

It's really worth it, working here for just a few days like this?

KEN. I could use the extra money. Even if it's just three days. And I mean I think it'll be good for me, I think – …

   (pause)

Grace, the woman I'm replacing, she just – left?

ETTA. Think she just found something else, like everyone did. It was amazing how fast everyone left, the moment they said we were being shut down there was this exodus.

   *(**GINNY** enters carrying a box. She goes to a corner with several packed boxes, places it with them, organizes a bit.)*

There used to be seventy or so residents here, after a few weeks it was down to just my husband Gerald and I, plus Tom. Only staff left are Faye and Ginny –

   *(**GINNY** half-waves at **KEN**, then exits.)*

– plus the one who hired you. Last soldiers left standing.

KEN. So – where will you go?

   (pause)

ETTA. We have a place set up at the Good Samaritan Village.

KEN. Oh right, the one over by the –. I bet it's nice there.

ETTA. Very well may be. But for Gerald it'll be a new place he doesn't recognize, a larger place, a more disorienting and certainly more frightening –. Well.

   (pause)

To be honest I'm not sure why it had to shut down, I think whatever corporation owned this place decided they could make more money selling it than they could –. They said it was about resident complaints, but that's just ridiculous. We had a couple of loudmouths from Montana in here (these people from Montana you'd think they'd be heartier) and they thought they were being treated poorly, something about –

(GERALD *enters, looks at* ETTA. KEN *looks at* GERALD.)

ETTA. Hi, Gerald.

KEN. *(to* GERALD, *loud)* Hi – I'm Ken? I'm going to be working in the kitchen for the next few days?

ETTA. He's not deaf, dear.

(to GERALD*)*

Do you need something, Gerald?

(GERALD *looks at her, searching.*)

GERALD. No, I –.

...

...

Uh.

(pause)

ETTA. This is Ken. Say hello to Ken.

(GERALD *nods at* KEN.)

He's replacing Grace for the next few days. You remember Grace?

(pause)

Grace, the cook. *Grace.*

GERALD. I'm not hungry, I –.

(GERALD *goes to a shelf with a small stereo on top, presses plays. From the stereo we hear Arvo Pärt's "Für Alina*," loud and tinny.* GERALD *listens.*)

(ETTA *turns to* KEN.)

KEN. *(awkwardly)* I'm – sorry.

ETTA. What for?

KEN. Sorry it just –. Sorry.

(pause)

---

*Please see Music Use Note on Copyright Page.

ETTA. He has some good days. Well, *had*. Good days are behind us at this point.

   (to **GERALD***)* Gerald.

GERALD. Hm?

ETTA. The music is so loud, please.

> *(***GERALD*** turns down the music.)*

He's nine years older than me, we were married when I was twenty-five, he was thirty-four. People would remark on the age difference, and we'd say, "Well when we're in our seventies or eighties it won't seem like much difference at all." Suppose we were wrong about that one.

GERALD. I don't –

   …

   …

I don't remember what I came in here for.

   …

I don't remember.

ETTA. I know, Gerald.

> *(***GERALD*** looks at* **KEN** *and* **ETTA** *for a moment, then leaves the room, leaving the music on.* **ETTA** *goes to the stereo, turns off the music.)*

KEN. It's really – beautiful.

ETTA. I'm sorry?

KEN. I mean –. You've been together so long.

ETTA. Oh.

KEN. You must love each other so much.

ETTA. He doesn't remember who I am anymore, dear.

> *(Pause.* **ETTA** *goes back to* **KEN***, sits down.)*

KEN. *(stricken)* Oh, wow… I'm *so, so sorry* –

ETTA. Oh, no, it's fine –

KEN. That's just *so sad.*

ETTA. Okay.

KEN. *It's so, so –*

ETTA. Alright you're going to have to stop that right now.

KEN. Sorry, I –. I don't know, not being able to recognize the person you *love* –

ETTA. I mean he was never too forthcoming with love anyway, I think he thought it was tacky, or –. Not that he didn't love me, he just didn't –. We had a short-hand for it. He never liked to say "I love you" before bed, he was embarrassed by it frankly, so we started just saying "See you in the future."

KEN. The – future?

ETTA. Yes, when we both wake up, the next day. "See you in the future." The future sounded much more optimistic back then, I suppose.

> (**FAYE** *enters with a box and earbuds in her ears.*
> *She puts the box with the others, organizes a bit.*)

You couldn't tell now, but he was a – brilliant man. PhD in Musicology, Professor Emeritus at the university. He always thought he was the smartest person in the room, most of the time he was right. He loved to put people in their place, he loved to make his points. Honestly he was never happier than when he was saying something about something.

> (**FAYE** *exits.*)

Someone your age, you should be working somewhere else. Somewhere a little less depressing maybe.

KEN. Well it's –. I just think it – could be good for me.

ETTA. Oh?

KEN. When I saw this job posting at first I wasn't even going to apply even though I could *really* use this money, but when I thought about it, I thought that maybe it could be a good opportunity for me to – ...

> (*pause*)

I think I just need to realize that, you know, dying isn't – bad. It's a good thing, it's kind of – beautiful.

> (*pause*)

ETTA. You think when I die, you think that's going to be "beautiful"?

KEN. Have you accepted Jesus into your heart?

ETTA. Oh honey.

> *(pause)*

Three days you'll be here, right? You can make it three days.

KEN. Sorry, that came out weird, I'm not trying to be –.

> *(pause)*

My pastor thought it was time for me to get out, to find work, interact with people more – and when I told him about this job, he thought it might be – *good* for me.

ETTA. "Good" for you?

KEN. Yeah. I sorta have a hard time with, like – death?

> *(short pause)*

ETTA. You really shouldn't have taken this job.

KEN. No it'll be good, I mean –. I'm reborn now, I'm finding peace, and maturity, and – I just need to realize that this a place full of people who are about to be reunited with God, that it's really a – *positive* thing. Right?

> **(GERALD** *re-enters, upset.)*

GERALD. *Every time that I –.*

> ...

Every time I go in there, you know.

> ...
>
> ...

Every damn time I go in there, the –. The people without faces at the end of the bed.

> ...

People without faces.

> ...

You know that?

(ETTA *goes to him, keeping her distance.*)

ETTA. Yes, Gerald.

GERALD. People without faces, at the end of the bed.

...

...

I said that there are people without faces.
At the end of the bed.

...

Looking at me without any eyes.

> (GERALD *stops, looks at* ETTA. *He slowly calms down. Silence.*)

I know you.

> (*pause*)

ETTA. Yes.

> (*They look at each other for a moment.*)

> (JEREMY *enters holding a few forms and an ID. He hands* KEN *the ID.* GERALD *makes his way out of the room.*)

JEREMY. (*to* KEN) Alright, here's your license back, I think we're good to go. Grace left us enough in the freezer to get us through the night, so. See you in the morning.

KEN. Great, thanks.

> (JEREMY *exits.* KEN *looks at* ETTA.)

KEN. It was really nice talking to you.

ETTA. You too, dear.

> (KEN *goes to the sliding glass doors, they open. He looks outside, hesitates. He turns back to* ETTA.)

Just a few days with us, honey. You'll be fine.

Scene Two

(Late morning, the next day. **TOM** *is sitting on a recliner closer to the television, which is on at a low level. It plays an emergency broadcast from a local station warning of a winter storm.)*

*(***GINNY*** *stands, watching the television.* **FAYE** *is at a window, nervously looking outside.)*

(A tense silence.)

FAYE. Do we know –, like, *when* he left? Did she say anything?

GINNY. No.

> *(The sliding glass doors open abruptly.* **FAYE** *and* **GINNY** *look at the doors expectantly.)*
>
> *(The doors remain open for a moment, then close. Short pause.)*
>
> *(***GINNY*** *turns back to the window.)*

FAYE. It's getting really bad out there.

GINNY. I'm sure someone's found him.

FAYE. If someone found him, wouldn't we have heard by now?

GINNY. When he did this last August, it took almost all day for him to walk into that Kmart and –

FAYE. Yeah in *August*, it's like twenty degrees outside, if he's out there it's not going to take long before he – …

> *(short pause)*

Okay, I'm sick of just standing around, maybe we should circle the building again?

GINNY. The police will be here any second, they're gonna be able to –

> *(***ETTA*** *enters, tense and worried.* **FAYE** *stops herself.* **ETTA** *glances at* **FAYE**, *then sits, half-watching the television.)*

(Silence. FAYE goes to ETTA.)

FAYE. I'm sure this is all going to work out.

ETTA. Hm.

FAYE. He's done this before, someone always finds him.

ETTA. Yes.

(KEN enters with a tray of snacks for TOM.)

(The sliding doors open again. Everyone stops, looks at them. Silence. The doors close.)

(KEN looks at FAYE, FAYE forces a smile back at him. KEN gives TOM the snacks, then exits.)

GINNY. You know I'm sure by this point he's found some house, or –. You know that trailer park is only about half a mile from here.

FAYE. That's true, and if someone saw him walking by they would / have –

ETTA. Yes thank you.

FAYE. And when the police get here, they'll be able to drive around and see if they –

ETTA. Thank you, yes. We don't need to talk about it, thank you.

(ETTA stops, struggling.)

FAYE. Oh, hon.

(FAYE gets up, goes to ETTA.)

ETTA. I'm sorry.

FAYE. You have nothing to be sorry about –

ETTA. I'm fine –

GINNY. Oh, hon.

ETTA. *Please* don't patronize me, I don't like it.

(JEREMY enters. ETTA begins to gather herself.)

JEREMY. *(to FAYE)* Have they called?

(sees ETTA)

Oh, honey –

ETTA. *Everyone stop.*

> *(Awkward silence.* TOM *finally looks away from the television, looks at* ETTA.*)*

TOM. Gerald wander outside again, Etta?

> *(pause)*

ETTA. Yes, Tom.

TOM. Can't find him?

ETTA. No, Tom.

TOM. Very sorry to hear that.

ETTA. Yes thank you.

> *(Silence.* TOM *goes back to watching the television.)*

JEREMY. *(to* FAYE*)* Nothing?

FAYE. No.

JEREMY. But why don't – ? Aren't there like, *emergency vehicles* or – ?

ETTA. Everyone please stop talking about it, it's really just not helping, I –.

> *(*ETTA *stands up, starts to exit and then turns back.)*

Look I realize that you're all being nice about this, but I have to say that the way you all express sympathy and concern, it's very annoying. I'm sorry if that's rude of me to say (I'm not really sorry actually) but it's the truth, it's really very annoying.

> *(*ETTA *exits.* KEN *enters, goes to* TOM.*)*

JEREMY. Shouldn't we be – doing *something?* I just feel like we should go out there, maybe one of us should do some driving around, or –. Ginny, did you bring the SUV?

GINNY. / Matt took it, I have the wagon.

KEN. *(to* TOM*)* You want anything else, Mr. M.?

TOM. Coffee?

KEN. *(to* GINNY/FAYE*)* Can he have coffee?

GINNY. He really shouldn't –. Oh fuck it, give him coffee.

FAYE. Ginny.

GINNY. Oh he can't hear me.

*(**KEN** exits.)*

What about the sons, should we call them?

FAYE. Yeah, I guess we should / probably –

JEREMY. *No,* we're not –. There's no reason to get family involved right / now –

FAYE. Jeremy, he's *missing* for Christ's sake –

JEREMY. He is not – ! Now we don't know that, he / could be –

FAYE. Of course we "know" that, he's not here and we don't / know where –

GINNY. Okay, okay –

(The sliding doors open again. They all look at them. Pause.)

JEREMY. *Jesus,* it's still doing that?!

*(The sliding doors close. **JEREMY** grabs a folding chair, sets it under the doors, starts fiddling with them.)*

You know I'm actually *glad* we got shut down, seriously. It's not worth having a heart attack before I'm fifty. The stupid plastic surgeons that bought this place, let them deal with this stupid door. See if they can –

*(**JEREMY** gets shocked by the door.)*

FUCK.

GINNY. Okay, I think we're done playing with the door. C'mon.

*(**GINNY** goes to **JEREMY**, helps him off the chair.)*

JEREMY. It shocked me!

GINNY. I know, honey.

JEREMY. It really shocked me. It really just did that.

*(The phone rings, **FAYE** goes to answer it.)*

FAYE. *(on the phone)* / Pine Manor Assisted Living.

JEREMY. I'm sorry.

GINNY. It's fine.

FAYE. *(on the phone)* / Yeah, we spoke earlier, I think.

JEREMY. Do you think I should call Eileen? She's gonna
chew me out so bad, I know she's / gonna –

GINNY. Nothing's happened to him yet, calm down.

JEREMY. I just don't –. I mean could we get in trouble for
this? Could we go to *jail* or something for this?

FAYE. / I understand that, but I'm just wondering what *we*
should be doing, like if there's something we could do
in the meantime, or – …

GINNY. Dear *God* Jeremy, we are / not going to –

JEREMY. Well it's not like crazy, right? We do have some
responsibility here, if it looks like we were just *hanging
out* while a resident with severe dementia just wanders
into the –

> *(The sliding door open again.* JEREMY *and*
> GINNY *look. A pause.* JEREMY *buries his face in
> his hands.)*

FAYE. *(on the phone)* Okay, thank you.

> *(The doors close.* FAYE *hangs up.)*

GINNY. *(to* FAYE*)* Anything?

FAYE. Branch Road is completely snowed in on the north
side. So they couldn't even look.

JEREMY. They *closed the road?*

FAYE. Guess they had to. They're gonna try swinging
around and taking the highway, see if they can come
from the other side.

JEREMY. Oh, God.

> *(*KEN *returns with coffee, gives it to* TOM.*)*

KEN. What's wrong?

FAYE. Branch is snowed in on the north side.

KEN. Whoa.

JEREMY. Okay, I can't stand just sitting around here, I'm going to go drive over toward the highway, see if I find him.

> (**JEREMY** *stands up, grabbing his coat from behind the reception desk.* **KEN** *exits.*)

GINNY. I don't know if that's a great idea, Jeremy, why don't you just circle the building a few more times, check the parking lot – ?

JEREMY. I've already done that, *someone* has to be out there looking for him –

FAYE. Jeremy, stop, does your Corolla even have four wheel drive?

JEREMY. Well I'll walk then!

FAYE. *Walk?* This is the worst blizzard we've had in years, you're not even wearing a hat –

GINNY. Look you're not in New Mexico anymore, this isn't exactly –

JEREMY. Stop it, stop treating me like I'm a kid or something just because I'm from New Mexico! I've been here for two years, I've seen snow, I know what I'm getting into, just –.

> *(pause)*

I *am* your boss, you know?!

> (**JEREMY** *moves to the sliding doors, they don't open. He waves his hand in front of the sensor, nothing happens.* **JEREMY** *seethes. He turns around, heads toward the back.*)

I'll go out the *fucking stupid* back door.

> (**JEREMY** *exits.*)

> *(Silence apart from the television.* **FAYE** *and* **GINNY** *look at one another.*)

FAYE. He's gonna get himself hurt out there.

GINNY. Oh let him get hurt then.

FAYE. No, really, maybe –. Maybe I should go with him.

(**FAYE** *grabs her coat.*)

GINNY. Faye, / don't –

FAYE. Look maybe he's right, maybe we should look for Gerald if the police can't get through –

GINNY. You can't see two feet in front of your face out there, you think you / can find –

FAYE. Well I'm sick of just sitting here not knowing if he's out there freezing to death or something –

GINNY. I guarantee you someone has already found him and / they are –

FAYE. No, you don't know that, Ginny, just let me –

(**GINNY** *goes to* **FAYE.**)

GINNY. Faye, you're *pregnant*, you can't just –

FAYE. *Ginny.*

(**FAYE** *motions to* **TOM**, *who continues to watch television.*)

GINNY. Oh he can't hear me, calm down.

(**FAYE** *relents, puts her coat back.*)

FAYE. I just can't stand thinking about him wandering out there. I know he's done this before, but with this storm, and all that farmland east of us –

GINNY. Even if he walked down the farm access road, which I doubt, there are cars coming down that thing every twenty minutes at least. Someone would have seen him. What's more likely is that he went walking toward town and someone found him after ten minutes.

(*pause*)

And even if – I mean I don't think he is, but even if – the man's over ninety for God's sake, and he's just getting worse – these past few months he's wandered outside at least five or six times, this was bound to –.

(*pause*)

Never mind. He's fine. I'm sure he's fine.

(FAYE takes a breath. Silence.)

GINNY. Why are you still so weird about me telling people?

FAYE. Oh my God.

GINNY. I just don't / know why –

FAYE. Okay, look, maybe we should be / focusing on –

GINNY. *Faye.*

(FAYE relents.)

FAYE. I just don't –. I don't see why we have to make some big *announcement.*

GINNY. No one's saying we have to make a big announcement, I just don't know why it has to be this big secret –

FAYE. Well maybe it's personal, maybe / it's –

GINNY. You're not *embarrassed*, are you? Matt and I aren't embarrassed, so / you –

FAYE. *No,* it's not that, Ginny, I –.

(pause)

It's just been – tough lately.

(pause)

GINNY. Yeah, hon, I know. I know it. But it's been a *year* now –

FAYE. I know, Ginny, but I just / feel like –

GINNY. You can make the decision to move on with the rest of your life, you know?

FAYE. I just – … Look I mean I only started working here to be around him more, and now that he's gone I feel like I – …

GINNY. I know, I was here too, I know what – … But you don't have to *wallow* in this, just –. There are good things in your life right now, just focus on the good things. Okay?

(Pause. FAYE looks at her.)

What?

(The phone rings. FAYE looks away from GINNY.)

FAYE. Okay.

> (**GINNY** *looks at* **FAYE** *for a moment longer. The phone rings again,* **GINNY** *answers it.*)

GINNY. *(on the phone)* Pine Manor, this is Ginny.

> (**JEREMY** *re-enters, red-faced, cradling his right hand.*)

FAYE. What?

GINNY. *(on the phone)* Yes, hi, have you – …?

FAYE. Jeremy, what?

JEREMY. Nothing, I –.

> *(pause)*

The back door is frozen shut and I got upset and hit it and I really hurt my hand I don't know if I broke it –

GINNY. / Well how long is this supposed to last?

FAYE. Okay, come here. Lemme look at it.

JEREMY. I just like hate myself sometimes.

> (**FAYE** *looks at* **JEREMY**'s *hand.*)

FAYE. No, you're –. I don't think it's broken, it doesn't look broken.

JEREMY. Seriously I hate myself so much sometimes, / I really –

FAYE. Okay take a breath. Sit down, you're okay.

> (**JEREMY** *sits down.* **KEN** *re-enters, goes to* **TOM**.)

GINNY. *(on the phone)* / Wait – so what does that mean, what are you saying?

KEN. *(to* **TOM***)* You all done, Mr. M.?

TOM. More coffee, please?

KEN. Oh I don't know, Mr. M., I don't know if we / should –

TOM. It doesn't do anything to me.

KEN. Um – Ginny? Is it okay if – ?

> (**GINNY** *waves* **KEN** *away.*)

GINNY. *(on the phone)* / Are you – ? You're sure?

KEN. Uh. Okay, I'll –.

> *(KEN exits.)*

> *(JEREMY and FAYE watch GINNY.)*

GINNY. *(on the phone)* Yeah, I understand that, but –
JEREMY. What is it?
GINNY. *(on the phone)* Well, no, probably not.

> *(pause)*

Okay. Okay, yeah.

> *(GINNY hangs up. She looks at everyone.)*

JEREMY. They find him?
GINNY. No, they uh. They didn't and – the highway's closed.

> *(pause)*

JEREMY. Wait, the *highway*?
GINNY. Fifty miles of it, anyway. They can't get out here.
JEREMY. What about the farm access road?
GINNY. It's all closed, Jeremy. Everything.

> *(pause)*

JEREMY. But so what are they gonna do, are they gonna – ?
GINNY. They can't, Jeremy. They just can't. Not until this passes, anyway.

> *(pause)*

They said to wait here, keep an eye out for him and – "hope for the best".

> *(Pause. KEN re-enters with coffee, hands it to TOM.)*

JEREMY. They said – ? They said "hope for the best", they really said that?

> *(Silence. The sliding doors open again, linger for a moment, then close.)*

Scene Three

(Early evening. ETTA *sits near the television, which is on at a low level. She barely pays attention to it, lost in thought.)*

*(*FAYE *enters, carrying a box full of medical supplies.)*

*(*ETTA *looks at her, smiles vaguely.)*

FAYE. Can I get you / anything?

ETTA. Oh, no, I –. People aren't still outside, are they?

FAYE. Jeremy and Ginny are circling the parking lot one last time before it gets too dark.

ETTA. They really shouldn't be out there in this weather, they – ...

(re: the medical supplies)

What's that?

FAYE. Oh, it's –. Honestly it's just a lot of junk. I feel so helpless, I had to do something. We're supposed to sort it, see what's worth selling to the hospital.

*(*FAYE *goes toward* ETTA, ETTA *peers into the box.)*

ETTA. Oh Lord, that's a catheter, isn't it?

FAYE. Yes, it is.

ETTA. And it's in there with a jar of *tongue depressors*?

FAYE. Yeah, Jeremy isn't very – organized.

ETTA. I feel sorry for him.

FAYE. Why?

ETTA. I mean he doesn't know what he's doing. Some parent corporation hires that idiot to run this place, you can't blame him.

FAYE. Mrs. Erickson –

ETTA. Well I don't mean it like –. I'm not trying to *insult* the poor idiot, I'm just saying.

*(*FAYE *laughs a little.* ETTA *smiles.)*

ETTA. I'm being so *rude* today, aren't I? I'm being so rude.

> *(pause)*

FAYE. Can I – ? Would you like me to sit with you?

> *(pause)*

ETTA. Now I hope you know I'm not looking for some pity party, I hope you know that.

FAYE. I'm not giving you one. Promise.

> *(Pause.* FAYE *sits down, looks at the television.)*

They saying anything new?

ETTA. No, not really. They're saying five feet, maybe six up toward Deary.

> *(*FAYE *takes a thermometer out of the box, looks at it.)*

Snow in our room was almost up to the window when I was in there. Oh Faye, is that a rectal thermometer? I hope you're going to wash your hands.

FAYE. I'm sure it's been washed.

> *(*ETTA *looks at her. Pause.* FAYE *considers, then puts down the thermometer.)*

Yeah, maybe I –.

> *(*FAYE *goes to the front desk, takes a bottle of Purell, squirts some into her hand.* ETTA *turns the television off.)*

> *(*FAYE *looks at* ETTA *for a moment.)*

Look, Mrs. Erickson, I'm just so sorry that –

ETTA. Oh here we go.

FAYE. What?

ETTA. I believe I told you *specifically* that I wasn't / interested in –

FAYE. *(unintentionally high-pitched)* I know honey, but I'm just sorry that –

ETTA. I swear, no one under fifty nowadays knows how to express sympathy in a way that's not completely condescending.

FAYE. Well you didn't even let me say anything.

(pause)

ETTA. Alright, have a crack at it.

(Pause. **FAYE** *looks at her.)*

FAYE. *(direct, simple)* I'm very sorry that you're going through this. I still have faith we'll find him, but nevertheless this must be difficult. And if there's any way I can help, please let me know.

(pause)

ETTA. That was better.

FAYE. You see?

ETTA. Your voice didn't go up into that sickly sweet register, it was much better.

FAYE. Thank you.

(pause)

ETTA. It's so odd not having him around, my days for so many years have been full of my desperate attempts to *orient* him. Every five seconds, "That's a picture of our son Benny, dear," "This is Tommy, he's here to change our sheets," "This is our room, there are two beds because we *both* sleep here." Maybe it's what kept me from senility, constantly reminding myself where I was, what I was – ...

(pause)

You've been here what, six years?

FAYE. Seven. Well, I guess almost eight.

ETTA. Do you think Gerald –, that he's gotten worse, this past year or so?

(pause)

In your opinion. I'm just curious.

(pause)

FAYE. Yeah, I mean –. I think so, yes. When I first got here he seemed to recognize me, but recently he –. And he seemed to be listening to his music more back then.

ETTA. Well he never really stopped that.

FAYE. Really?

ETTA. The only part of his brain that refused to shut off. Even after every other part of his mind seemed to fall away, he never lost the music, I could always cling to that one last part of him. Not surprising, I suppose. It takes a pretty strong will to grow up in rural Wyoming and decide to become a musicologist specializing in post-modern sacred choral works.

FAYE. I guess I never knew much about him, I knew he was a music teacher at the university and / that he –

ETTA. Music *professor*. In his better days he would have really gone after you for calling him a music teacher, music *professor*. University of Idaho gave him tenure faster than you could believe. Taught as long as he could. The university was good to him, I'll say that much. But after a while –. He'd miss a class now and then, students would complain, the dean tolerated it. But about twelve years ago, he walked into a lecture hall, turned on a recording of the Latvian Radio Choir performing Arvo Pärt's "Berliner Messe" (his favorite, he listened to it constantly), and sat listening to it silently for about ten minutes before touching himself inappropriately in front of fifty or so horrified freshmen.

FAYE. Oh.

ETTA. Yes, *oh*, I think we all breathed a collective *oh* when that happened. The signs were there before that, of course, but we dismissed them, *I* dismissed them.

(pause)

If he knew what he had turned into, he would –. He'd be so humiliated.

(pause)

FAYE. Have you talked to Dave and Benny yet?

> *(pause)*

ETTA. Well, they –.

> *(pause)*

Look to be honest I haven't called them yet, but I don't want to hear anything about it.

FAYE. You haven't – ?

ETTA. I said I don't want to hear anything about it.

FAYE. I didn't say anything, I just –. I thought maybe you'd want to let them know –

ETTA. Oh I just don't see any reason in getting them all worked up, they're so sensitive, especially when it comes to their father. They'd have Gerald hooked up to an iron lung before they were ready to say goodbye to him, I'm telling you. If I tell Dave he's missing he's liable to snow-shoe in here from Minneapolis, it's not –. There's just nothing they can do, there's nothing any of us can do, we can't – …

> *(ETTA struggles.)*

Excuse me.

FAYE. Oh honey –

> *(ETTA glares at her. Silence. ETTA takes a deep breath, FAYE doesn't know what to say.)*

ETTA. Alright, enough.

FAYE. What?

> *(ETTA goes uptstage to a box, rummages around a bit, pulls out a bottle of port.)*

ETTA. This has been collecting dust on our bureau since the millennium (it's not even good or anything) and I don't feel like taking it with me.

> *(ETTA grabs two paper cups from reception, goes to FAYE.)*

FAYE. Oh, you go ahead, I'm fine.

ETTA. Oh just a little.

FAYE. I think it would put me to / sleep, I –

ETTA. A little bit won't hurt the baby, you'll be fine.

> *(pause)*

FAYE. I'm sorry?

ETTA. I said a little bit won't hurt it. People are so sensitive about that nowadays, when I was pregnant I drank and smoked the / whole –

FAYE. How did – ? How did you know about – ?

> *(pause)*

ETTA. Oh you're – ? I'm sorry I'd assumed you'd be telling people by now.

FAYE. Did Ginny tell you?

ETTA. Faye, I was a receptionist at a doctor's office for thirty-four years, I know what –. I mean you haven't even had coffee.

> *(**ETTA** pours a normal glass for herself, a small glass for **FAYE**.)*

Look a lot of women nowadays are having babies without getting married, it's nothing you have to worry about. Not with me, anyway. I hope I didn't embarrass you, I didn't mean to embarrass you.

> *(pause)*

FAYE. No, it's – fine.

> *(pause)*

It's not, um. Well it's not really – mine?

> *(pause)*

ETTA. I'm sorry?

FAYE. I'm having it for Ginny.

ETTA. "For Ginny"?

FAYE. I mean not like – wow, you'd think I'd have figured out how to explain this by now. A few years ago, Ginny had pelvic cancer, and because of the radiation she can't –. Anyway, this year she and Matt have been talking about a kid, finding a surrogate, so I – …

    (pause)

ETTA. Offered.

FAYE. Yeah, I –. I offered.

ETTA. Huh.

    (pause)

Did you do the – ? The in vitro / fertilization – ?

FAYE. No, it's –. It's mine, biologically.

    (pause)

But I mean it's not *mine*, it's Ginny's.

ETTA. Well of course it's yours dear.

    *(Silence. **FAYE** and **ETTA** drink.)*

FAYE. I mean she's my best friend, she's been my best friend since high school and I knew what she was going through, and – … And they're giving me some money, which believe me is going to be helpful, especially since I'm losing my job, and – … But it's not just that, after this last year, I just wanted to do something – forward-looking, something – …

    (silence)

It's just been a – weird year for me. Losing Dad and everything.

ETTA. Yes, I'd imagine.

FAYE. I mean the entire reason I became a CNA and started working here was so I could take care of him after his diagnosis, and now – …

    (short pause)

Sorry, I don't / need to –

ETTA. No, Faye, it's fine, you –.

    (pause)

Up until now I just assumed you didn't want to talk about it. When he passed, there was such a – tremendous silence surrounding it.

FAYE. Yeah, there was. Still is.

> *(pause)*

ETTA. When his cancer had gotten worse, those last few months, / did you – ?

FAYE. You know I actually don't –. I'm not sure if I can talk about it, I don't know if I – ?

ETTA. I'm sorry –

FAYE. No, it's –.

> *(awkward pause)*

Sorry, this is all to say – I guess I thought having a baby would be doing something *good*, something life-affirming. Something – about the future.

> *(pause)*

ETTA. I see.

> *(pause)*

Does it feel that way?

> *(Pause.* **FAYE** *looks at her.)*

> *(***GINNY*** *enters wearing a coat and holding a flashlight, sees* **FAYE** *with the port. Pause.)*

GINNY. What are you – ?

> *(pause)*

FAYE. Oh, it's just –

GINNY. You're drinking?

FAYE. We were just –. We were just having a little drink. I just had barely a sip.

ETTA. I pushed it on her, I take full responsibility.

> *(silence)*

FAYE. Ginny, I really wasn't –

GINNY. Maybe that's not a good idea.

> *(Silence.* **FAYE** *puts the cup down.* **GINNY** *puts the flashlight down, takes off her coat, hangs it up.)*

FAYE. Did you find anything?

GINNY. No, we –. Back door's still frozen shut. It's impossible to see anything out there, anyway.

> (*pause*)

Ken said dinner's gonna be a little late. Another forty-five minutes or so.

> (*pause*)

FAYE. Okay.

> (**GINNY** *exits. Pause.*)

> (**ETTA** *picks up the bottle of port.*)

ETTA. I'm sorry, I shouldn't have pushed this on you, it was –.

> (*pause*)

I'll put it away.

> (**ETTA** *starts making her way out of the room.*)

FAYE. I think I –. I've made a mistake –

ETTA. It was just a little sip of port wine, it's not –

FAYE. I don't mean that, I mean –.

> (*pause*)

I don't think I should have done this, I don't know what to – …

> (**FAYE** *trails off. Silence.*)

ETTA. This baby? You're talking about the baby?

FAYE. I'm sorry, I don't know / why I'm –

ETTA. You're worried about giving it up? You're worried you'll want to keep it?

FAYE. No, it's not that at all, I'm just worried that I –. I'm worried that I shouldn't be having a baby *at all*, like – how much shit is going to happen to them, how much will they suffer, all because I needed money and Ginny wants to feel needed, and –.

> (*pause*)

FAYE. God, I sound so awful. I hear what I'm saying, it sounds so awful.

(silence)

ETTA. We do place an inherent value on life, don't we? Life, in and of itself, is always good, no matter what. So we're told.

(Pause. FAYE looks at ETTA.)

FAYE. I mean, do you think that Gerald – ?

(FAYE stops herself, looks away.)

ETTA. What?

FAYE. No, forget it.

ETTA. Ask me.

(pause)

FAYE. I really don't want this to sound –. I don't want to offend you, but –

ETTA. You're wondering if Gerald might be better off if he...?

(pause)

I don't know. I don't know what to think. To be honest I've never felt more helpless and lost in my entire life.

(pause)

You're making a life. Creating something new. Take comfort in it. Try to take comfort in it.

(TOM enters, heads straight to the television and turns it on.)

FAYE. I'm gonna see if Ken needs help with anything.

(FAYE exits. ETTA looks at the television, goes and sits with TOM. The broadcast continues to talk about the storm.)

(Silence as they watch the television.)

ETTA. No end in sight to this, huh?

TOM. They all end eventually.

ETTA. Hm.

>   *(Silence. They watch.)*

TOM. Etta.

>   *(no response)*

Etta –

ETTA. Yes, Tom, I know.

>   *(pause)*

I know.

Scene Four

(Shortly later. KEN *is at the window, nervously staring outside.* JEREMY *enters with a clipboard.)*

JEREMY. Hey / I was –

KEN. *(startled)* AH –

JEREMY. GEEZ –

KEN. Sorry, / sorry –

JEREMY. Calm down, it's me, it's / just me –

KEN. I'm sorry, I just –.

> *(pause)*

Sorry.

> *(pause)*

JEREMY. You worried about the storm?

KEN. No it's not that, I actually like it, I was –. I was trying to calm myself down by watching the snow.

> *(pause)*

I'm sort of an anxious person?

JEREMY. Yeah, I –. I see that.

> *(pause)*

So listen, I know you're still cooking but when you're done I was thinking you could inventory what's left of the kitchen supplies?

KEN. Yeah, I can do it. Sorry.

> *(pause)*

JEREMY. You worried about Gerald, is that what's going on?

KEN. Yeah, I guess, but not in the right way?

> *(pause)*

I was in the kitchen, and the vents were on and they're kinda loud, and I realized that someone could be like right behind me and I wouldn't know it, and I kept thinking that I'd turn around and someone would be –. I just wanted to come out here where it was quieter, where someone couldn't sneak up on me.

JEREMY. Guess that didn't work.

KEN. No, it –.

    (pause)

Look this is gonna make me sound terrible, but I have this fear that I'm gonna turn around and Gerald will be standing there, or worse his *body* will be – …

    (pause)

JEREMY. That's like a really weird fear.

KEN. Yeah I – … I don't know I'm sort of weird with this kind of stuff, I took this job because my pastor thought it would be good for me, and – …

    (pause)

What made you start working here?

JEREMY. What do you – mean?

KEN. I mean did you want to have a closer relationship to the elderly, or did end of life care appeal to – ?

JEREMY. I got divorced.

KEN. Oh.

JEREMY. Yeah, I just needed a –. I don't know, I needed to get outta there.

    (pause)

We were only together for like eight months, but it was a *lifetime.* Those eight months were like a *lifetime.*

    (pause)

KEN. How did you guys meet?

JEREMY. Match dot com.

KEN. That's really beautiful.

    (pause)

JEREMY. And now I'm in Idaho, and I don't have a job, and I have no idea what the fuck I'm going to do.

    (pause)

KEN. I mean listen, I think we all have our own paths. I think God has a plan for you, maybe you just don't know what it is yet.

(pause)

JEREMY. If God has a plan for me, then he like *really* hasn't thought it through very much.

(pause)

Wait, so – why did your pastor want you to work here?

KEN. Oh, I just –. I sort of get overwhelmed easily, especially when it comes to death and dying, and… My pastor just thought that maybe, working here, I'd gain a – positive relationship with death.

JEREMY. I mean, I don't think most people have a super positive relationship with death.

KEN. Yeah, but I, like – …

(pause)

My stepdad OD'd on our kitchen floor when I was ten, I found him. He had been dead for hours. Growing up my mom wasn't super – stable, and this last year things have gotten worse for her, so finally I just had to leave and – …

(short pause)

Anyway, things have been a lot better lately! I got out of there, moved here, and this church in town has been good for me, Pastor Jake is really – … And I just think that God's plan can sort of be surprising. Sometimes he puts us on paths that we don't really expect.

(silence)

JEREMY. Yeah so like if we have some spatulas, then you can write "spatulas" in the first column there and the second column you can –

> *(A kitchen timer in* **KEN***'s pocket goes off. He pulls it out, looks at it.)*

KEN. Meatloaf's done.

JEREMY. Oh.

KEN. I'll get started on the inventory after dinner.

JEREMY. Cool.

> (KEN *takes the clipboard from* JEREMY, *starts to exit toward the kitchen.*)

Ken?

KEN. Yeah?

JEREMY. You, like – have a place to stay and everything, right?

KEN. There's a couch in the church basement.

JEREMY. Oh.

> (*short pause*)

Is it – okay?

KEN. I mean it's better than my car.

> (KEN *smiles at* JEREMY. *Pause.*)

JEREMY. And you really think that there's still a plan for you?

KEN. I mean – sure. God led me here for some reason – right?

> (GINNY *enters with an old card table.*)

GINNY. Jeremy the dining room is *freezing* –

JEREMY. Well yeah, I turned the heat off last night –

GINNY. Where did you expect us to eat for the next two days?!

JEREMY. They told me to cut corners, you think I should heat a two-thousand square foot dining room for / three people?!

GINNY. Okay just get the folding chairs, please?

JEREMY. *God. Fine.*

> (JEREMY *exits.* KEN *goes to* GINNY, *they try to stand the card table up unsuccessfully.*)

KEN. This leg is broken I think –

GINNY. No, there's a trick to it, I just don't remember what –.

(FAYE enters with a packed box.)

GINNY. *(to FAYE)* You remember how to this?

(FAYE puts the box down, goes to GINNY.)

FAYE. It's the one leg, you have to like pop it out or it won't –

(FAYE messes with one leg of the card table, they manage to stand it up.)

(KEN heads toward the kitchen.)

KEN. Meatloaf's done, so we're ready I think.

GINNY. Okay.

(KEN exits.)

(Silence. GINNY and FAYE stand together awkwardly.)

FAYE. Listen, Ginny, I'm sorry about earlier?

GINNY. Oh, no –

FAYE. Really, I / owe you –

GINNY. Honey I've thought about it and I was totally overreacting. I mean it was just a little sip of wine, / how could it –

FAYE. Well that still doesn't / make it –

GINNY. It's not a big deal. But listen, can we – …?

(pause)

Are we – okay?

(Pause. TOM enters.)

TOM. Dinner?

GINNY. On its way, Mr. M.

(TOM sits on the recliner, GINNY turns back to FAYE.)

FAYE. Ginny –

GINNY. I know this is a lot for you to take on, but I just – , something's up and / I don't –

FAYE. I'm fine.

TOM. I would like my dinner now.

GINNY. *(to* **TOM***, loud)* It's coming Tom, can't make it come any faster.

> *(to* **FAYE***)*

Faye, I'm sick of feeling like I've lost my best friend or something and not knowing / why –

FAYE. I don't / know if I –

GINNY. If it's me, if I said something or did something then / you can –

FAYE. *No*, it's not you, it's – …

> *(Silence.* **FAYE** *considers. She looks at* **GINNY***.)*

You're still happy about this baby, right?

> *(Pause.* **GINNY** *looks at her.)*

GINNY. What?

FAYE. I mean, when we decided to do this, it felt so – *beautiful*, I felt like I was doing something so special for you and Matt, like I was helping you create this life, it felt so – …

> *(pause)*

But when we did the ultrasound last week, and we actually *saw* the baby for the first time, you asked me how I felt and I told you I felt so happy, but – … I didn't feel that way. I'm not sure what I felt, but I – … I mean I *am* happy, but – …

> *(pause)*

I'm not explaining myself very well.

> *(Silence.* **GINNY** *looks away, goes back to the table.)*

What?

> *(no response)*

You asked me what was wrong.

GINNY. And you told me.

> *(pause)*

FAYE. Alright, Ginny, you're not allowed to *force* me to tell you what I'm feeling and then get mad at me / for –

GINNY. Well I didn't think that you were gonna tell me you don't want to have this baby all of the sudden.

FAYE. Okay, I didn't say that –

GINNY. I thought you were gonna say you were worried it would be hard to give the baby up, or you're tired or morning sickness, or –. *Normal pregnancy things.*

FAYE. Look it's not like I'm not going to go through with it, I'm just telling you –

GINNY. "Not going to go through with it"? What does that mean, why did you just say that?

FAYE. I *said* it's *not* like I'm *not* going to go through / with it –

GINNY. But you've thought about it.

FAYE. No! Of course not!

GINNY. If you think that *that* is an option here –

FAYE. Oh my God, Ginny –

TOM. I am very hungry right now, I would like / my –

GINNY. SHUT UP, TOM.

FAYE. *Stop. Ginny. Stop.*

> *(Silence.* **GINNY** *breathes, trying to calm herself down.* **FAYE** *goes to* **TOM.***)*

Mr. M., it's on its way, I promise. Okay?

> *(***TOM** *nods at her,* **FAYE** *goes back to* **GINNY.***)*

Nothing's happening with the baby. It's gonna be healthy, I'm gonna have it, you guys are gonna raise it, just like we've talked about. Okay?

> *(pause)*

You asked me what I was feeling, and I told you. This isn't about some big crisis, this isn't about –. This is just about something I'm feeling. That's all.

> *(pause)*

GINNY. So what you're feeling – is that you wish you hadn't have done this.

> *(Pause.* **FAYE** *doesn't respond.)*

> *(***JEREMY*** enters with folding chairs.)*

JEREMY. No place settings?

GINNY. I'll get some.

> *(***GINNY*** brushes past ***JEREMY***, exits.)*

JEREMY. What?

FAYE. Nothing.

JEREMY. Did I say something?

FAYE. No, Jeremy.

> *(pause)*

JEREMY. Were you talking about me?

FAYE. *No,* oh my God.

> *(***KEN*** re-enters with a large pan of meatloaf, he heads toward the table.* **GINNY** *follows after him with place settings.)*

KEN. I got this recipe from a lady at my church, if it's half as good as she makes it then you guys are gonna love it.

> *(***FAYE*** goes to ***GINNY***.)*

FAYE. Ginny –

> *(***GINNY*** ignores ***FAYE***.)*

GINNY. *(calling out)* Etta. Dinner.

> *(***GINNY*** exits, ***FAYE*** watches her leave.)*

> *(***KEN*** starts to carve up the meatloaf.)*

KEN. Mr. M., you wanna stay there or you wanna come eat with us at the table?

TOM. I'm fine here.

JEREMY. *(to* **FAYE***)* Any calls?

FAYE. No, sorry.

> *(***KEN*** brings meatloaf to ***TOM***.)*

KEN. How's the storm looking?

TOM. Bad. Bad, bad, bad.

KEN. I have potatoes too, I'll get them.

    (KEN exits, ETTA enters.)

ETTA. What is it?

TOM. Meatloaf.

ETTA. Ech. Are there potatoes?

FAYE. Ken's getting some.

    (GINNY re-enters with a pitcher of water.)

Here I can get that –

    (GINNY ignores FAYE, brushes past her, puts the pitcher of water on the table. Throughout the following, no one pays any attention to anything that TOM says.)

I can get / the cups –

GINNY. I'm fine.

    (GINNY exits down the hall again.)

JEREMY. What's wrong?

FAYE. Nothing, it's fine –

JEREMY. Seriously is this about the stupid dining hall? If I leave the heat on in the entire building / then the –

FAYE. *(a little too severe)* Oh for Christ's sake, Jeremy –

JEREMY. / *Sorry*, sorry –

ETTA. You know what? Why don't we finish that bottle of port, why don't we have that with dinner.

    (ETTA gets up, heading toward the bottle of port.)

TOM. I'd like some.

ETTA. It's not very good, but –

    (KEN almost runs into ETTA as he returns with the potatoes.)

/ Eh eh eh –

KEN. Sorry, sorry –

(**ETTA** *exits.*)

(**KEN** *heads to the table with the potatoes.* **GINNY** *re-enters with cups, sits at the table.*)

KEN. We didn't have a lot of butter, I hope they taste okay.

FAYE. / I'm sure they're fine.

GINNY. *(to* **JEREMY***)* You talked at all with the police / about – ?

JEREMY. Not for a couple hours.

GINNY. Should we call them or something?

JEREMY. I mean they'd call if they heard anything.

GINNY. God I feel so *powerless*, I can't stand it.

(**ETTA** *re-enters with the bottle of port, she starts pouring people drinks.*)

TOM. / This meatloaf has no salt.

KEN. Oh you know what we need a serving spoon?

JEREMY. You know where they are?

KEN. Yeah I think so hold on –

(**KEN** *exits.*)

FAYE. *(whispering, to* **GINNY***)* Look I'm sorry –

GINNY. *(ignoring* **FAYE***)* Etta, I'll have some.

ETTA. I'm sure everyone's in the mood / for a little.

FAYE. I'm fine, thank you –

JEREMY. Go ahead, have some.

FAYE. No, thanks, I can't.

TOM. / This meatloaf has no salt in it.

JEREMY. You "can't"?

FAYE. I mean I'm fine.

JEREMY. If you're in recovery or something maybe we shouldn't –

FAYE. / No, I'm not –

GINNY. She just doesn't want the wine, Jeremy, leave it alone.

(KEN re-enters with a serving spoon, puts it in the potatoes.)

KEN. / Okay! Are we all good?

TOM. It's because she's pregnant.

FAYE. I think so, Etta you want some water?

ETTA. No, thank you, I'm fine.

(Everyone is seated, about to eat.)

KEN. Maybe we should say a prayer.

(pause)

I mean for Gerald. Maybe it would be nice to say a prayer for Gerald?

(Pause. Everyone looks at ETTA.)

ETTA. Yes, I –. I suppose that would be nice, I think that's very appropriate.

(KEN looks at JEREMY. Pause.)

JEREMY. What?

KEN. Would you like to – ?

JEREMY. Me? Oh – I mean I'm not –. I'm probably not the one to do this, I'm really not religious. I've never like – prayed before.

GINNY. You've never *prayed?* Everybody's *prayed.*

JEREMY. My parents thought organized religion was evil, I mean they took me to chanting circles a couple times but they never really, like –

ETTA. Yes I would like Jeremy to do it.

(Pause. Everyone awkwardly lowers their heads.)

JEREMY. Um. So... I would – *we* would just like to ask you to return Gerald to us. Please give him back to us, please find it – in your wisdom? – to deliver him. To us.

(pause)

Please keep him safe, and – nourish him? – with food, and with – drink.

(pause)

JEREMY. *(cont.)* And please God, help us.

> *(pause)*

Please help us. Please God help me.

> *(People open their eyes, looking at* **JEREMY**, *who continues.)*

(losing it a little) Please God help me. Please just –. *Please help me.*

> *(pause, regaining himself)*

And thank you for the –. For the food.

> *(pause)*

Amen.

> *(Everyone starts to eat.)*

KEN. *(to* **JEREMY***)* Did that feel good?

JEREMY. It was – fine.

KEN. You know God is always there if you need help, he's / the –

FAYE. *(re: the meatloaf)* Oh Ken there's no salt in this.

KEN. What?

FAYE. I think you forgot the salt.

KEN. Really?

> *(***KEN** *tastes the meatloaf.)*

JEREMY. Yeah it's like dog food, it tastes like dog food.

KEN. I'm so sorry –

ETTA. It has a nice flavor, it just needs some salt –

KEN. I'll go get it, I'm so sorry –

> *(***KEN** *exits to the kitchen.)*

ETTA. It's still better than Grace's cooking, I'll say that.

FAYE. Oh she wasn't that bad. She made those shrimp thingies?

ETTA. I know you liked her, but I / swear –

GINNY. So I have some good news for everyone.

> *(pause)*

JEREMY. Oh yeah?

GINNY. I know it's a strange time to bring it up, but I guess we could all use some good news right about now, right?

FAYE. Ginny, what / are you doing?

GINNY. So for a while now, Matt and I have been talking more and more about becoming parents, but it's complicated because I'm actually not able to have a baby of my own. But this past year we both realized that we really want a kid, so we decided to find a surrogate.

FAYE. / Ginny –

GINNY. And it's Faye. Faye's going to have our baby.

(pause)

JEREMY. Oh wow –

GINNY. And she's in her second trimester, so we're going to start telling people.

*(to **FAYE**)*

Yeah?

(pause)

FAYE. Yeah.

JEREMY. Well that's –. I mean, congrats! That's really great.

GINNY. Thanks. I know, weird timing, but. Just thought it would be nice to share some good news.

*(**FAYE** looks at **GINNY**. Pause.)*

*(**KEN** re-enters.)*

KEN. Sorry guys, I only found one shaker and it's empty? Do we have any more?

(no response)

Guys?

FAYE. Yeah, I can show you.

*(**FAYE** exits with **KEN**.)*

(Awkward pause at the table.)

ETTA. Well. Congratulations.

GINNY. Thank you.

ETTA. Second trimester, well. Is it a boy or a girl?

> *(pause)*

GINNY. We, uh. We don't know.

ETTA. You want to be surprised?

GINNY. I guess so, I mean Matt and I – ...

> *(pause)*

I guess we just didn't really talk about it.

> *(pause)*

ETTA. Boys are easier. Which do you want?

> *(pause)*

GINNY. I don't know.

ETTA. Boys are easier. Hope for a boy.

> *(Pause. The sliding doors open, linger for a moment, then close. Another pause.)*

JEREMY. Are you giving Faye money for it?

> *(pause)*

GINNY. We're –. Yes, she gets a – fee, that's how it's usually done.

JEREMY. Oh. That's –.

> *(Pause. **JEREMY** drums his fingers on the card table.)*

> *(silence)*

How much you paying her?

> *(**ETTA** and **GINNY** don't look at him. Another silence.)*

Geez I can't like say *anything*.

> *(**FAYE** and **KEN** re-enter, with salt. **KEN** holds a bottle of sauce.)*

KEN. I also found some barbeque sauce if anyone wants to –

(**KEN** *stops, looking out the window.*)

GINNY. What?

(*pause*)

Ken?

(**KEN** *moves to the window, looking out.*)

What?

KEN. I just –.

(*pause*)

I thought I saw something. Like a – person. I thought I saw a person out there.

FAYE. Are you sure?

KEN. Well no, but I –. I really think I just saw someone out there –

(**JEREMY** *and* **GINNY** *go to the window, looking.*)

(*pointing*) Right there, see?

(*pause*)

I swear I saw someone standing there, I saw – I thought I saw someone standing and then fall down.

JEREMY. Where?

KEN. At the end of the field, like – like past the farm access road, near the base of the mountain.

(**KEN** *goes behind the reception desk, taking his coat.*)

I'm gonna go see, I just want to make sure it's not him.

(**TOM** *looks at* **ETTA**.)

ETTA. Now Ken, I really –. I really don't think he's out there –

KEN. Well I'm probably wrong but I just want to check –

GINNY. That's gotta be half a mile away, you gonna be okay walking in this? The police said we shouldn't be / outside in this –

KEN. I'll be careful, I just want to make sure that it isn't –

> (**KEN** *goes to the sliding doors, standing in front of them. They don't open.*)

TOM. / Etta?

KEN. How do I? How do I make it open?

> (**KEN** *tries to pull the door open.*)

Is it locked or something?

JEREMY. Oh, I don't know, Trent always took care of this stuff, I don't know / how to work it –

KEN. Look if that's him he needs us *now*, he might be freezing to death –

JEREMY. Well I don't know!

> (**KEN** *kicks the door.*)

TOM. *Etta.*

KEN. What about the back door?

GINNY. That's been frozen shut for hours –

KEN. Should I just / break it open or something?

GINNY. Alright, there's a crowbar in in the utility closet –

JEREMY. / You guys can't pry open the door you'll break it!

KEN. Where?

GINNY. The closet toward the back of the / hallway –

ETTA. NO, PLEASE JUST – ...

> (*Pause. Everyone stops.* **ETTA** *is shaking, visibly upset.*)

He's *not out there,* I promise you, he's – ...

> (*pause*)

FAYE. Etta, what?

> (*pause*)

What is it?

> (*Silence. Finally,* **TOM** *stands up, facing everyone.*)

TOM. You can all calm down.

> (*pause*)

Gerald's in his bedroom.

(pause)

He's in his bedroom.

(black)

End of Act One

ACT TWO

Scene One

(Shortly later. **JEREMY, KEN, FAYE, GINNY** *and* **TOM** *all stand or sit near* **ETTA,** *who sits nervously in a chair.)*

(The storm has gotten worse, the wind outside howls every so often. Snow is now up to the base of the windows.)

(A long, tense silence.)

FAYE. So you – ... Last night, you just – decided?

(Silence. **JEREMY** *buries his face in his hands.)*

JEREMY. Oh my God. Oh, my God.

(pause)

ETTA. You all have to understand for the last twelve years – *twelve years* – his mind has just – evaporated. Daily routines, memories, faces, eventually whole sections of his life, friends and family and –. And now, with the prospect of moving him into a new facility, a new confusing landscape, more unfamiliar faces –

GINNY. If you were worried about moving, you could have talked to us / about –

ETTA. There's nothing you could have done, this is what I'm saying, there's nothing anyone could have done.

JEREMY. / Oh my God.

GINNY. We could have worked this out, we could have *talked about this –*

ETTA. And what would you have told me? "Hang in there," "We all love Gerald," "Stick by the people you love," you'd just throw these – *slogans* at me like I was looking for a morale booster or / something –

FAYE. *Okay*, guys, just – …

> *(Another silence. The sliding doors open, linger for a moment, then close.)*

GINNY. Did Tom – did he *help* you do this, / or – ?

ETTA. *No*, of course not, I –. I just didn't know what to do after it was over, I needed to talk with someone, figure out what to do – and we decided that we would at least just wait until morning, that I would tell you all that he had died in his sleep, but in the middle of the night I realized that they might be able to tell, that if they did an autopsy or something they might realize that / I –

FAYE. But why didn't you just *tell* us, you let us spend all day thinking that he had wandered off / outside –

ETTA. Now this is the thing, I *never* told you that he wandered off, you just saw me in the morning and when I told you I didn't know where he was, you – … I mean he had done this so many times before, wandered outside, you all just assumed he'd done it again and I – … Look, I know that I should have told you right then but I just had this moment of *panic*, I didn't know what to do, how to tell you what I had done –

GINNY. But why last night? He's been like this for years, what happened last night?

> *(pause)*

ETTA. I'm not proud of keeping this from you all as long as I did, but before I could figure out how to handle this you were all convinced he had gone outside, and I know I should have said something hours ago, but / I just –

KEN. How did you do it?

> *(Pause.* **ETTA** *looks away.)*

TOM. Lock on the medication locker has been broken for weeks, you all know that.

>*(pause)*

He just – drifted off. It was very peaceful.

>*(Silence. Everyone breathes.)*

GINNY. Jeremy how long have I been telling you about that stupid medication / locker –

JEREMY. So this is *my* fault?! *You're* responsible for medication on the night / shifts –

GINNY. Well I'm not responsible for the / fucking *locks* on the –

FAYE. / Okay, guys –

JEREMY. *And* you're the one who searched the patient wing this morning, you didn't think to check his *bedroom?*

GINNY. Why the hell would I check his bedroom?! Etta said he was gone, you think I'm / gonna barge into their bedroom and –

FAYE. *Okay guys enough, just –* … Just stop.

>*(Pause.* **TOM** *moves to the card table, sitting down, serves himself a slice of meatloaf and pours some salt on it.)*

Etta, you realize – … You know this is, this is something you could get in serious trouble for –

ETTA. Why do you think I waited this long to say anything? Of course I / know that –

JEREMY. Okay, okay, everybody just –.

>*(pause)*

I need to think.

>*(pause)*

Fuck.

GINNY. Etta, have you – … Have you told Dave and Benny?

ETTA. What?

GINNY. Dave and Benny. Did you tell them that you – did this?

ETTA. Of course I didn't, they'd never forgive me, they'd never…

(*Pause.* **GINNY** *looks at everyone.*)

GINNY. So – we're the only ones who know about this.

(*pause*)

JEREMY. Wait, *yeah* –

FAYE. What do you mean?

GINNY. I'm just saying there's a way to handle this, maybe, without making a big / deal about –

JEREMY. *Yeah, we can* – we can tell them that we finally found Gerald in an empty room, that he hadn't gone outside after all, and we / just –

ETTA. I'm sorry, I can't –. Excuse me.

(*pause*)

I'm so sorry everyone.

(**ETTA**, *overcome, makes her way to her room.* **FAYE** *looks at* **GINNY** *and* **JEREMY.**)

FAYE. Nice, guys.

GINNY. We didn't / mean to –

JEREMY. Look, sorry, I just mean – I doubt they're gonna do some extensive autopsy or anything, I mean it's not like we have a fancy coroner, Clive is just some – guy, I think he's an accountant or something, he's not / like –

FAYE. This is crazy, we can't just pretend / that he –

JEREMY. Okay fine, we call the police and tell them – what? That one of our residents decided to *murder* her husband?

FAYE. No, because that's not what happened –

GINNY. With everything that's happened here, I just don't see why we can't make this – simple. I know it's weird, but would it really change anything?

JEREMY. *Exactly*, Gerald's – gone, he's gone, and nothing we say or don't say is going to change that, and I for one don't want to get involved in some messy legal whatever, and I certainly don't want to see Etta get in trouble for God's sake. I mean really, what's the difference?

KEN. But we can't – , I mean we – …

(Pause. **FAYE,** **JEREMY** *and* **GINNY** *look at* **KEN.***)*

Look I know I'm new here, I know that I don't have the experience or whatever, but –. I don't know if I can just *pretend* that I don't know what really happened.

(pause)

JEREMY. Ken, Gerald was ninety years old –

TOM. Ninety-one.

JEREMY. Ninety-one years old, his own wife says that there was barely any of him left, this isn't some cold-blooded –

KEN. I know, but it's not – … I mean he was alive, he looked at me, we *met* each / other and he –

(The sliding doors open.)

GINNY. Ken, we've all been dealing with Gerald for a very long time, / he really wasn't –

KEN. *I know,* but he's not – …

(The sliding doors close.)

All I'm saying is that, it – *he* mattered, *his death* matters, and / we can't just pretend that –

GINNY. / Of course it does –

JEREMY. / Oh for Christ's sake –

KEN. *I just* –. I just don't know if I can lie about it.

*(*KEN* looks at* FAYE. *Pause.)*

FAYE. I don't – …

(pause)

God, I don't know. I don't know what to do.

JEREMY. / *Seriously?*

GINNY. Guys – Gerald started going downhill *twelve years ago,* and Etta's right, it would have been awful for him to move into Good Sam's this / late in the game –

JEREMY. / Exactly –

FAYE. But is that reason enough to just – get *rid* of him?

JEREMY. / She wasn't "getting rid" of –

KEN. I mean look, I know I don't know anything about this, and I know that he's been like this for a while, but I can't just act like what she did last night / was okay –

GINNY. But it's done! It's already done, we can't change that, what happened last night doesn't matter, / what we're talking about is –

FAYE. / Doesn't "matter"?

JEREMY. / Okay –

GINNY. I don't mean that, I just mean –

(The sliding doors open.)

JEREMY. Okay, I am not debating this with some *kid* that I hired to be our cook for three days –

FAYE. Okay, / okay –

(The sliding doors close.)

JEREMY. No, I'm serious, I am the boss here, and I say that we are going to tell the police that we found Gerald / in the –

KEN. Look you can't *make* me say something that's not true –

JEREMY. / Well then just don't say anything, how about – ?!

FAYE. / Jeremy, you're not helping –

GINNY. Ken, we're not asking you to lie –

TOM. OKAY.

(Everyone falls silent, looks at **TOM.** *Pause.)*

Okay.

(pause)

Five or six years ago, for some reason you all got the idea that I was deaf. I went along with it because, frankly, not being expected to engage with you people suited me just fine. But, unfortunately, my hearing is as good as it's ever been, and I've been listening to all of you go on and on, and I know you'd like to think that I don't have an opinion but I do. And here it is: shut up.

(*pause*)

Shut your mouths.

(*pause*)

You're all so obsessed with this idiotic *debate*, with the moral whatevers of your own tiny little universes, but you know what actually matters? There's a broken woman who just lost her husband, and she needs your help. Therefore: stop making this about yourselves. Shut up.

(**TOM** *makes his way out of the room, taking his plate of meatloaf with him.*)

(*The doors open, linger for a moment, then close. Pause.*)

GINNY. Alright, let's –. Let's at least deal with this body that we have down the hall?

(*pause*)

JEREMY. Okay.

GINNY. 19 is empty, right?

JEREMY. Yeah.

GINNY. Okay, we can put him in there, I'll crack the windows so the room is cold, we don't want him to start –.

(*pause*)

You can go get him?

JEREMY. Yeah, we'll –. Ken, help me get him, okay?

KEN. Oh, I –.

(*pause*)

I don't really do so well around dead bodies? I don't / know if –

FAYE. Okay, Jeremy, I can help you, just –

KEN. No, no, I –.

(pause)

KEN. I'll do it.

FAYE. You sure?

KEN. Yeah.

(pause)

Sorry.

*(Everyone starts to make their way out of the room.
KEN stops.)*

Look, I'm sorry for – like, lecturing you guys or
whatever. I just wanna make sure that –. I want to make
sure we feel okay about this.

(pause)

I'm going to pray about it, okay?

(pause)

Do me a favor, just – pray about it.

Scene Two

(Later that night. **TOM** *drinks coffee and watches the television which plays a late-night program at a very low-level.)*

*(***ETTA*** *enters holding a notepad. She looks at* **TOM**.*)*

TOM. You doing okay?

ETTA. Yeah, I just –. I can't sleep, I tried for hours. I've been up trying to be productive, I thought I'd start on his obituary. I've barely written anything, I don't know what –.

(pause)

You can't sleep either?

TOM. I worked a night shift for forty-two years. I sleep when my body needs sleep.

*(***ETTA*** *sits down.)*

ETTA. What were they all saying about me?

TOM. People say what people say, Etta. Doesn't matter.

ETTA. Do they think I'm crazy?

TOM. I don't know.

ETTA. Do they think I'm a murderer?

(The television suddenly turns to static.)

TOM. Damn.

*(***TOM*** *grabs the remote, changes the channels a few times. It's all static.)*

Well that's that, isn't it?

*(***TOM*** *turns off the television.)*

When I first got here, I used to do these jigsaw puzzles, you remember that? There was this television here but I was determined to do something more constructive, something less passive. So I'd do these damn jigsaw puzzles all the time, filled most of my room with them.

TOM. *(cont.)* Spent years doing it. Eventually I look around my room and realize I've spent years reconstructing photographs and paintings that a company had disassembled for me. Never felt more like a rat in a cage in my entire life.

> *(pause)*

Turning on the television seemed strangely like a more productive activity.

> **(TOM** *gets up, takes his coffee cup to a trash can and empties it into the can.)*

Gerald was a music teacher, that's right?

ETTA. Professor.

TOM. Professor, sure. Music professor. I was a night watchman at a grain tower complex outside Boville for most my life. Never understood why it even needed a watchman, as if someone is going to come and steal two tons of lentils or whathaveyou in the middle of the night.

> **(TOM** *goes to a water cooler, fills his coffee cup with water.)*

Point is, my life has been fairly mechanical and simple, and I'm not complaining, I've had a full life. Two beautiful daughters, many wonderful years with Dorothy before the leukemia. But for Gerald, a music professor, I suppose that was more the life of the mind. So when you lose the mind, I suppose there's not much life left?

> *(pause)*

Anyway, I'm no philosopher.

> **(FAYE** *enters, starts cleaning up the table.)*

> **(ETTA** *looks at* **FAYE.** *Pause.)*

ETTA. I can't imagine what you must be thinking of me right now.

FAYE. Etta, we –. Look we were all surprised, but it's not like we all don't – understand where this is coming from. I think the important thing for us is just to make sure that you're going to be okay.

ETTA. What did you – ? What did you end up doing with him?

FAYE. Ken and Jeremy took him to an empty room.

(pause)

ETTA. What room?

(pause)

FAYE. Do you really want to – ?

ETTA. I won't go stare at him or anything, I just –. I would like to know what room he's in.

(pause)

FAYE. 19, I think.

ETTA. Marcy's old room?

FAYE. Yeah.

ETTA. Marcy's old room. Alright.

(silence)

TOM. Television's out now, phones might follow soon. Last I heard the snow'll let up in the morning, so.

(**TOM** *makes his way down the hall.*)

Goodnight, then.

(**TOM** *exits. Silence.*)

FAYE. *(re:* **ETTA**'s *notebook)* What's that?

ETTA. Oh, I figured I should write his obituary, start to write it anyway. I've barely written anything.

FAYE. You want some help?

ETTA. Well, I –

FAYE. Seriously, I can't sleep either, I don't mind.

(short pause)

ETTA. Okay.

(ETTA *sits down, hands* FAYE *the notepad.* FAYE
sits as well.)

FAYE. *(reading)* "Dr. Gerald Alan Erickson, 91. Born May
26th, 1922. Professor and father."

(*pause*)

That's all you have?

ETTA. I just don't know what I'm supposed to, you know. I
don't know how to do this, I just don't care about these
things –

FAYE. Well it's okay, why don't – ? Just start chronologically,
where was he born?

ETTA. Oh he wouldn't want to bother with that, he hated
where he came from. A farm outside some tiny little
town in Wyoming, he never talked about it.

FAYE. Okay, you –. Maybe – his parents' names?

ETTA. He never got along so well with them, he'd want that
out.

(*pause*)

FAYE. Okay, then – you could list where he got his degrees?

ETTA. Well that's sort of dry, isn't it?

FAYE. It was important to him though, right?

ETTA. Absolutely not, he believed college was a big
scam. Used to say that going to a library was a better
education than any university could give you.

FAYE. He taught at a university and he felt that way?

ETTA. Gerald was a – unique animal, we'll say that. He
didn't want to have some normal job, he wanted to
spend his days doing the only thing that was important
to him, so he found a way to do it. Doesn't mean he
had faith in it. He was a terrible teacher, everyone said
it. Brilliant man, terrible teacher.

FAYE. Okay, there's –. I mean it's sort of standard, but
you could say something like, "devoted father to two
/ boys – "

ETTA. Eh.

(pause)

FAYE. What?

ETTA. I mean, "devoted"? I don't –. I mean I suppose you could put that in.

(pause)

FAYE. He wasn't – ?

ETTA. I mean he was fine, he was a fine father, he paid the bills, he showed them affection when they needed it, but "devoted"? He was a normal father.

FAYE. So brilliant man, terrible teacher, normal father. That's what we have so far.

ETTA. Well see this is my point, this is why I'm having trouble! He's not – an easy man to encapsulate, I'll say that much. Two paragraphs to sum him up sort of contradict his entire personality, he was the antithesis of brevity.

(pause)

FAYE. You can always tell people where they could send flowers or cards. Do you know what your unit number at Good Sam's is going to be? You could include that?

ETTA. Oh, well, I don't –. I'm not so sure about that now.

(pause)

FAYE. What do you mean?

ETTA. I mean they had us all set up for this two person unit, so I'm not even sure if they'll have a place for me –

FAYE. I'm sure they'll be able to accommodate you –

ETTA. And to be honest I'm not even sure I want to go over there, you know that terrible Trisha woman who worked here a few years ago? I heard she got hired over there, and I / don't –

FAYE. Well so what – ? What are you going to do?

ETTA. Well, for the last fifty-odd years of my life I haven't had much of a say in where I was going to live, or how I was going to –.

(*pause*)

There's this little town in Iowa, this little town called Tiffin where I was born, that was full of these Mennonites. We lived in this little one-story house that was near the only grocery store in town, and there was nothing but sprawling farmland in every direction, and the winters were so bitter and the summers were so wonderful.

(*pause*)

I haven't been there since 1978, you believe that? Gerald didn't much care for family history, he never really understood why I had this urge to go back. Maybe there's some little house like the one I grew up in, someplace close I can rent. Buy a little car, garden during the spring and summer.

(*pause*)

FAYE. You –. You're going to move to Iowa?

ETTA. I mean it sounds ridiculous, I know it sounds ridiculous, but –. I mean I don't know what else is keeping me here.

(*Pause.* **FAYE** *puts down the notebook, stands up, paces a bit.*)

What?

(*pause*)

FAYE. You're moving to Iowa?

ETTA. Well it was just a *thought*, I don't know, I –

FAYE. You think you're going to be able to live by yourself, you won't need anyone around to –

ETTA. Well Faye honestly you and I both know that the reason I'm living in this place doesn't have anything to do with *me*, it was all about –.

(Silence. **FAYE** *looks away.)*

Alright now, I know you're thinking something, just come out and / say it –

FAYE. So you're free now.

(pause)

ETTA. I'm "free"?

FAYE. That's sort of how it sounds, sounds like you've freed yourself from something, shook off the dead weight, or –.

(pause)

I don't mean that, I didn't mean it like that. But it does almost seem like you're – *happy* about this.

(Pause. **ETTA** *stands up.)*

ETTA. I'm going to my room.

FAYE. No, wait –

ETTA. I don't know what it is you're / trying to do –

FAYE. Look I just –. If you're going to have us all – *cover* for you like this, I need to know that –. I need to know that you did this for Gerald, that you were helping him, that you weren't just –

ETTA. You're a girl. You're a silly girl.

(pause)

You have no idea what that man was / going through –

FAYE. You've said that before, and I hear you. We all hear you, I can imagine how hard it was for him, and for you –

ETTA. No, actually, you *couldn't* imagine it, you couldn't *begin* to imagine it, I / promise you –

FAYE. Okay, you know what? You don't have a monopoly on grief! And you certainly don't seem too broken up about losing him, so I don't / know why –

ETTA. Do you think last night was *easy* for me?! You of all people should understand this, the way your father suffered those last few years, the / way he –

FAYE. He *did* suffer, but you know what I did?! I *fought* with him, we both fought as hard as we could, because *that's what you do.*

> *(Pause. **ETTA** looks at **FAYE**.)*

ETTA. I see, now we're getting to it. That's is what this is all about?

FAYE. Okay, nevermind, it doesn't even / matter now –

ETTA. What I did last night – you think I made that decision *lightly?*

FAYE. No, what I'm saying is maybe that decision was wrong, maybe it was *vulgar.* I fought with my dad as hard as I could because those last few years were *worth it*, they / were –

ETTA. *(losing herself a bit)* Were they? I saw what happened to him later on, throwing up every night, his leg amputated. Did your father think it was worth all that suffering, or was that just you?

> *(Pause. **FAYE** looks at her. **ETTA** breathes, calming down.)*

I'm sorry.

> *(**FAYE** begins to head out of the room.)*

FAYE. Alright, I think we're done with the fucking heart-to-heart –

ETTA. *Stop.*

> *(**FAYE** stops, not looking at **ETTA**.)*

Faye, you – …

> *(pause)*

Obviously there's no way I can make you understand what happened last night, but you must realize – you have no idea what this has been like for Gerald, *or* for me. You're at the beginning of your entire life, you're having a baby, you / don't –

FAYE. *It's not even my baby.*

> *(pause)*

And trust me I'm not so happy about having my whole
life in front of me because right now it's looking pretty
long and lonely, and I – ...

(*pause*)

Shit.

(*silence*)

ETTA. Keep going.

(*Pause.* FAYE *looks at her.*)

FAYE. I mean at least when he was still here, I had some
reason to wake up in the morning, but when he died
I looked around and realized – I never even *wanted*
to be a CNA, I never wanted a job like this, now I'm
just *constantly* surrounded by people who are sick and
dying, and – ...

(*Pause.* FAYE *becomes more and more upset.*)

ETTA. And?

FAYE. And I have no idea what to do now, and I'm so
terrified that I'm just having this baby to try to make
myself feel better, for *completely* selfish reasons, and I
don't think that's fair to Ginny, *or* this kid, and – ...

(*pause*)

ETTA. And?

FAYE. *And,* I – ... I am *so fucking terrified* of the rest of my
life. I think about the rest of my life, and I'm *terrified.*

(*Silence.* FAYE*'s entire body is tense.*)

ETTA. Okay.

(*pause*)

Breathe, Faye.

(FAYE *takes in a breath, relaxing.* ETTA *goes to
her.*)

Better?

(*pause*)

FAYE. I –

> (*Suddenly the power goes out, the stage goes completely dark. A loud beeping is heard.*)

ETTA. What's – ?

FAYE. Uh – okay, just stay there –

ETTA. What's that noise, why is it doing that?

FAYE. I don't know, just – just stay there until I can find a flashlight –

> (**FAYE** *tries to get to the front desk, she trips and nearly falls to the floor.*)

Shit –

ETTA. What is it?

FAYE. It's fine, I just –. I rolled my ankle –

> (**ETTA** *tries to get to* **FAYE.**)

ETTA. Well here, let me –

FAYE. *No*, Mrs. Erickson, please stay there –

> (**KEN** *enters quickly.*)

KEN. Guys what's going on?! What do we do?!

FAYE. We just lost power, calm down, it's / not a big –

KEN. (*growing more frantic*) Is it going to come back on? When is it gonna come back on?

> (**JEREMY** *enters.*)

JEREMY. What the hell is / that beeping?!

FAYE. I don't know, I –. Jeremy, can you help me, I think I sprained my ankle or something –

KEN. Are you okay?!

JEREMY. Here, just a second –

> (**JEREMY** *makes his way to the front desk, finds a flashlight.* **TOM** *and* **GINNY** *enter,* **GINNY** *uses the flashlight on her cell phone.*)

GINNY. Everyone okay?

JEREMY. Yeah, just –

(GINNY sees FAYE.)

GINNY. What?

FAYE. Nothing, I just hurt my / ankle it's not –

JEREMY. Why isn't the emergency generator on? God is *everything* broken here?!

(GINNY goes to FAYE, helping her.)

KEN. Guys I'm really uncomfortable, this is really difficult for me –

(TOM makes his way to the source of the beeping, unplugs a small box from an outlet. The beeping stops.)

ETTA. Oh, thank God.

TOM. We have candles?

JEREMY. Yeah, in the kitchen closet. Ken, can you go get those?

GINNY. *(to FAYE)* / Can you put any weight on it?

KEN. Uh, I don't –. I don't know if I can –

FAYE. *(to GINNY)* / I think so, I think it's fine –

JEREMY. *Jesus Christ,* fine I'll get them!

(JEREMY exits to the kitchen.)

(TOM helps ETTA to a seat, they both sit down.)

GINNY. *(to FAYE)* Here, let's get it elevated –

(GINNY helps FAYE to a seat, brings another chair to elevate her ankle.)

(KEN grows more and more frantic.)

KEN. Guys, I don't –. This is bad, this is really bad.

FAYE. Ken, don't worry about it, we have candles and / plenty of water –

GINNY. Don't we have that old portable generator in the basement?

ETTA. Oh we won't need that, this likely won't last more than the night –

KEN. GUYS I JUST –.

> *(pause)*

Sorry but I –. I can't really handle the dark.

GINNY. You don't need to be scared, just stay in here with us –

KEN. NO I MEAN I CAN'T –. I don't know if I can be here, seriously, I really hate the dark, and especially in a place like this, and there's a body down the hall –

> (**JEREMY** *re-enters with candles and some lighters. He lights one, puts it toward the center of the room.*)

JEREMY. Where's that portable generator? Don't we have a portable generator?

GINNY. In the basement I think.

FAYE. We don't have gas though, do we?

JEREMY. We can check, there might be some down there. Ken, c'mon.

KEN. What?!

JEREMY. Come with me to the basement, we'll see if the portable generator is down there –

ETTA. Now honestly I think / we can survive one night without power, don't you think?

KEN. No, I can't, I really don't think I can go down there right now, I don't think I can –

JEREMY. / Okay I got the stupid candles, and I am *not* carrying up that generator all by myself –

FAYE. *(to* **ETTA***)* What about heat? We might need to plug / in some space heaters, or –

ETTA. *(to* **FAYE***)* We have blankets, we'll be okay with –

KEN. *(exploding)* NO I CAN'T DO THIS, I CAN'T BE HERE RIGHT NOW, I CAN'T –.

> *(short pause)*

GUYS I'M SORRY I DIDN'T TELL YOU THIS BEFORE BUT I HAVE THESE EMOTIONAL PROBLEMS –

(KEN starts to hyperventilate, he goes down to the floor, putting his head in between his knees.)

(GINNY goes to the floor, putting a hand on KEN.)

GINNY. Okay, shh –

(KEN flinches, GINNY takes her hand away.)

FAYE. *(to KEN)* What's gonna make you feel better? Can you tell me what'll help?

(FAYE goes to KEN.)

KEN. I DON'T KNOW THAT'S THE PROBLEM –

FAYE. Okay, okay you –. Just – breathe with me, okay? Just breathe –

(FAYE breathes slowly in and out, it's not helping KEN.)

Ken, can you just calm down a little and breathe?

(KEN continues to hyperventilate. GINNY goes to him.)

GINNY. We could say a prayer? You like that, right? Would that help?

(pause)

KEN. I DON'T KNOW MAYBE – ?

FAYE. Okay yeah, that's good. Let's try praying. Okay?

(Pause. GINNY thinks.)

GINNY. Dear Lord. We ask you now, that you could –. That you could come into our hearts, and comfort us. That you could – bring us peace.

FAYE. We ask that you – deliver us from this, that you turn the power back on, and make this storm go away.

(KEN's breathing starts to become a little more normal.)

And we ask that you –.

(pause)

We ask for your help. All of us, we ask for your help. We're – sort of small, insignificant people with small and insignificant lives and we're asking you for some help with that because we don't really know what to do here. We don't really know what to – …

(Pause. **GINNY** *and* **FAYE** *look at one another.* **KEN***'s breathing calms slightly.)*

GINNY. And we ask that you'll give us – confidence, that you'll give us confidence that we will all – know what's right. That you'll help us to do right.

(pause)

FAYE. That you'll help us to do right. That you'll help us to do the right thing with GERALD – and with everything else.

*(***KEN***'s breathing is now almost normal. He rocks back and forth a little.)*

(silence)

KEN. …please help us…

(pause)

…lord, please help us…

(silence)

*(***KEN***'s breathing finally becomes normal.)*

ETTA. Amen.

Scene Three

*(Much later, in the middle of the night. The wind
has become slightly calmer, the lights remain
off.* **FAYE** *sits on the couch with her leg elevated
slightly.)*

*(***TOM*** *lies asleep on a recliner,* **ETTA** *near him
asleep on a couch.* **JEREMY** *is asleep on the floor
under some blankets, facing upstage.* **KEN** *is also
asleep somewhere on the floor,* **GINNY** *is asleep in
a chair.)*

*(***FAYE***, unable to sleep, slowly reaches for a lighter.
She lights a single candle, looks at it.)*

(silence)

GINNY. *(softly)* You can't sleep?

(pause)

FAYE. Nah.

(Throughout the scene **GINNY** *and* **FAYE** *speak in
very hushed voices: a near whisper. Silences and
pauses are long and still.)*

GINNY. How's the – ?

FAYE. It's – fine. I'm not sure if I even sprained it. It's not
that bad.

(pause)

GINNY. You took some Tylenol?

FAYE. Yeah.

*(***KEN*** *mumbles in his sleep a bit, turning over.*
GINNY *moves onto the couch with* **FAYE***, sitting a
few feet away from her.)*

(silence)

GINNY. I caught Matt masturbating a couple days ago.

(pause)

FAYE. Oh.

GINNY. To porn, on his laptop.

> *(pause)*

By the end of the conversation I was the one apologizing, I have no idea how we got there.

> *(silence)*

FAYE. I'm sorry –

GINNY. It's okay.

FAYE. It wasn't fair of me to unload that on you, I / didn't –

GINNY. Faye I got mad at you because I'm not sure I'm completely confident about this baby either. I got mad because I was hoping that between the two of us you'd be the more optimistic one.

> *(pause)*

Matt spent almost eight thousand dollars re-doing the basement so he can have a room where he can play his video games. He knows that I'm about to lose my job, he knows we have a baby coming soon, and he just dropped *eight thousand dollars* re-doing the basement. I think it's mostly so he has a place where he can masturbate. He put a lock on the door a couple days ago.

> *(pause)*

He's probably masturbating right now.

> *(pause)*

Right this second.

> *(**ETTA** snores a little, shifting a bit.)*

> *(silence)*

He'll be a good dad though, yeah?

> *(pause)*

I mean a kid would like him.

> *(silence)*

FAYE. I actually think he's going to be a really good dad.

(pause)

GINNY. Really?

FAYE. Yeah. Really. He's fun, and he's caring, and –.

(pause)

And I mean having a kid could be good for him.

GINNY. Force him to grow up you mean.

FAYE. I didn't mean that –

GINNY. You did but that's fine, maybe you're right.

(pause)

God what an awful little hope to cling to.

(silence)

(**FAYE** *looks out the window.*)

FAYE. It stopped snowing.

GINNY. It did?

(**FAYE** *and* **GINNY** *both look out the window.*)

FAYE. That's good.

GINNY. Yeah.

FAYE. Maybe it's slowing down.

(silence)

GINNY. You know when we were juniors in high school, I went with Dean and those guys to John's Alley. Did I ever tell you that?

FAYE. You went to John's Alley in *high school?*

GINNY. You know Dean, he knew everyone there, they didn't –.

(pause)

Anyway I got very drunk very quickly, and before I knew it Dean was trying to take me back to his car, and I didn't –.

(pause)

GINNY. *(cont.)* Your dad was driving by. He pulled over, grabbed me, dragged me into his pickup. I was so mad at him, I couldn't even –. At one point he stopped the pickup, and he looked at me and he said, *"you are a smart and decent person."* And he took me home. Never even told my folks.

>   *(pause)*

I never thanked him for that.

>   **(GINNY** *shivers a bit, pulling a blanket around herself.)*

>   **(FAYE** *moves over to* **GINNY,** *putting a blanket around the two of them. They sit in silence for a moment.)*

FAYE. Matt's a good guy.

GINNY. Yeah?

FAYE. And he's going to be a good father. And you're going to be a good mother.

>   *(pause)*

GINNY. I hope so.

FAYE. You are.

>   *(pause)*

And this is a good thing.

>   *(pause)*

This is only a good thing.

>   *(silence)*

>   *(Then suddenly:)*

JEREMY. *(without moving, still facing upstage)* Guys I'm really scared about the future.

>   *(pause)*

I don't have a job and I don't know why I'm in Idaho.

>   *(silence)*

FAYE. You'll be okay, Jeremy.

JEREMY. I don't know.

GINNY. It's gonna be okay.

JEREMY. I don't know. I'm really scared.

> *(pause)*

I'm really scared.

> *(pause)*

FAYE. Jeremy, c'mere.

> **(JEREMY** *gets up, going to* **GINNY** *and* **FAYE.** *He sits in between the two of them,* **FAYE** *and* **GINNY** *spread a blanket over all three of them.)*

> *(silence)*

JEREMY. Do you guys think I'd be good at architecture? I've always thought I'd be good at architecture.

> *(pause)*

Maybe I should do architecture.

> *(pause)*

Or like work at Macy's.

> *(pause)*

GINNY. My friend Diana works there.

JEREMY. Really?

GINNY. Yeah. She's a manager. I could call her if you want.

JEREMY. I actually think I have a really good eye for fashion.

> *(pause)*

Could you tell her that?

GINNY. Yeah, sure.

JEREMY. Okay.

> *(pause)*

Okay well – that's something.

> *(pause)*

That's something. That makes me feel a little better.

(The sliding doors open suddenly, everyone wakes up with a jolt. They all look.)

(The doors linger for a moment, then close.)

Scene Four

(The following morning. Sunlight streams through the window.)

(Power has been restored, **TOM** *sits on the recliner watching the television.)*

*(***ETTA*** *sits with* **FAYE,** *holding the notebook from before.)*

ETTA. I mean I thought about it, and I'm sure it doesn't really exist anymore. Not the way I remember it, I mean. I imagine it's all been built up now, Walmarts and Applebees and everything else, I doubt my house is even still there.

FAYE. So you're – not going to go?

(pause)

ETTA. You know I'm just not sure, I think maybe packing everything up and just going out there is foolish and naïve, but I think maybe it's worth a visit at least.

(pause)

Do you think it's worth a visit?

FAYE. I think you should visit.

(pause)

Iowa's close to Minneapolis, you know. You could be closer to Dave.

ETTA. Oh he'd love that, wouldn't he.

*(***KEN*** *enters with food.)*

KEN. Eggs!

FAYE. Sounds good.

KEN. I used salt!

*(***KEN*** *brings a plate to* **TOM,** *exits.)*

ETTA. Alright. I should make some phone calls, I have to call this funeral director and let him quote me some very unreasonable prices for caskets.

FAYE. Did you ever – ? Did you think more about the obituary?

ETTA. Yes. Yes, I did, gave it some thought.

FAYE. Do you want any help with it, or – ?

ETTA. No, I believe I have it, I think I'm happy with it.

FAYE. That's good.

> *(pause)*

Can I read it?

> *(Pause.* **ETTA** *looks at her, relents. She hands* **FAYE** *her notebook.)*

(reading) "Dr. Gerald Alan Erickson, 91 – "

ETTA. Oh we're reading it out loud, is that really what we're doing?

> *(pause)*

Fine then.

> *(pause)*

FAYE. *(reading)* "Dr. Gerald Alan Erickson, 91. Born May 26th, 1922. Professor Emeritus of Arts and Sciences at the University of Idaho. Devoted father to – "

> *(stops reading, smiles at* **ETTA***)*

"Devoted" father?

ETTA. Oh shut up, give it to me.

> *(***ETTA** *grabs the notebook away from* **FAYE***.)*

(reading, somewhat quickly) "Devoted father to two boys, David and Benjamin Erickson of Minneapolis and Cleveland, respectively. Dr. Erickson received his Bachelor of Arts at the University of Wyoming, and a Ph.D in Musicology from Cornell University.

> *(***GINNY** *enters, unseen by* **ETTA***.* **TOM** *and* **GINNY** *start to listen to* **ETTA***.)*

Specializing in post-modern sacred choral work, and most recently interested in the work of composer Arvo Pärt, Dr. Erickson had the opportunity three times in his life to meet the composer, which he considered to be some of the greatest moments of his life."

(*pause*)

"Introverted and deeply personal, Dr. Erickson remained a mystery to most people who had only short interactions with him. To some, his manner could even seem off-putting or cold. But to those closest to him, to those who knew him best, he was a deeply heartfelt man whose towering intellect was matched only by his capacity for love."

(**ETTA** *pauses, collecting herself. She takes a few breaths, then reads.*)

(*simply*) "Dr. Erickson is survived by his wife, Etta."

(*Pause.* **ETTA** *puts the notebook down.*)

That's it.

(*pause*)

It's okay?

(**KEN** *enters.*)

KEN. More eggs! And toast!

(**KEN** *bring the eggs to* **FAYE,** *the toast to* **ETTA.**)

(**JEREMY** *enters.*)

JEREMY. Just got off the phone, they're on the way.

FAYE. What did you tell them?

JEREMY. All that worrying, I barely had to say anything, I just said we were mistaken, that he hadn't gone outside, that he had wandered into a room and just –. They didn't ask much.

GINNY. So they've opened up the highway?

JEREMY. Just to emergency vehicles, but they said later today they're planning on opening it up for everybody.

GINNY. Oh thank God.

(**ETTA** *heads down the hall.*)

KEN. Mrs. Erickson, you don't want to eat?

ETTA. I'll be hungry in a minute, I have to call this funeral
director.

FAYE. Etta, you know –. You know they're going to be here
any minute, to get Gerald.

 (pause)

If you don't want to be around we understand, we just –

ETTA. Frankly I'm not certain I want to be here when they
wheel him out of here.

 (pause, then to everyone)

I don't know how to properly say thank you for
something like this, but just –. Thank you.

 *(ETTA exits down the hall. GINNY sits down with
 FAYE, FAYE picks at her eggs.)*

KEN. *(to GINNY)* You want something to eat?

GINNY. Oh no, I think I'm okay.

KEN. Jeremy?

JEREMY. Um, sure. I guess.

KEN. Cool.

 (KEN turns, starts to head toward the kitchen.)

JEREMY. Uh, Ken – ?

 *(KEN stops, turns to JEREMY. JEREMY goes to
 him.)*

So are you – ? I mean, I didn't tell them anything, you
know. I didn't tell them what actually happened.

KEN. I know.

JEREMY. Are you – okay with that?

 (pause)

KEN. I think –.

 (pause)

I think God has a specific way of working, and sometimes
I just don't have a say in it. That's what I think.

 (pause)

JEREMY. Okay, I guess –. I guess I get that.

>*(pause)*

Hey, and you know, you – ... I mean, I know you have a place to stay at the church or whatever, but like –. I mean if you ever need a place to stay, I have a futon.

KEN. Oh, wow, thank you.

JEREMY. It's super uncomfortable.

KEN. Oh.

>*(Awkward pause. KEN nods at him, continues toward the back.)*

JEREMY. Oh, and – ...

>*(KEN stops, looks at JEREMY.)*

I just want you to know, I'm not like – *anti*-religion or anything.

KEN. Oh, sure.

JEREMY. I mean I'm not like –. I've just never been to –.

>*(pause)*

The church you go to, it's here in town?

KEN. Yeah.

JEREMY. Oh.

>*(pause)*

So like, what's it called?

KEN. It's called Mountain Fellowship? They're on Hillcrest, near the subdivision?

JEREMY. Oh that new church? The one that went up this year?

KEN. Yeah.

JEREMY. That's cool. I like that building.

>*(pause)*

KEN. Oh.

>*(silence)*

You know, you –.

(pause)

KEN. *(cont.)* I mean you could come sometime?

JEREMY. Oh.

KEN. I mean we're not like –. We really believe that people should come because they *want* to, we're not like knocking on doors and evangelizing all the time like some churches. But like, if you *wanted* to?

JEREMY. Yeah, maybe, I –. Maybe.

(pause)

But listen I think evolution is totally like a *fact* and that gay people are awesome and so I wouldn't / want to –

KEN. No that's fine, it's – we're not like that. Really.

(pause)

JEREMY. Oh.

(pause)

Cool.

KEN. Cool.

*(**KEN** smiles at him.)*

TOM. Coffee please?

KEN. It's brewing Mr. M., I promise. I'll be right back.

*(**KEN** exits toward the kitchen.)*

*(**JEREMY** joins **TOM** in front of the television.)*

JEREMY. *(to **TOM**)* What's on?

TOM. Divorce court show. Show where they're in a court and people are getting divorced.

JEREMY. Nice!

*(**JEREMY** and **TOM** watch the television.)*

(silence)

GINNY. *(to **FAYE**)* How're you doing?

(pause)

FAYE. Okay.

(pause)

Not sure.

(pause)

You?

*(Pause. **KEN** re-enters with coffee for **TOM**, gives it to him.)*

GINNY. Not sure either.

(pause)

We'll see what happens, I guess.

*(**GINNY** and **FAYE** look at one another. **KEN** goes to the table, starts to clean up dishes. Then, something catches **FAYE**'s eye down the hall. She stands up.)*

What?

*(**FAYE** exits down the hallway.)*

*(**GINNY** looks down the hall, sees something, then slowly stands as well. **KEN** looks down the hall, stops.)*

*(From the hallway **ETTA** and **FAYE** emerge, wheeling a hospital bed. **GERALD** is on the bed, motionless, covered in blankets.)*

*(**JEREMY** sees the bed and stands up as well. **TOM** sees it, turns off the television, stands.)*

*(**ETTA** and **FAYE** wheel the bed to the center of the stage, then stop.)*

(silence)

ETTA. I thought I, uh.

(pause)

I decided I wanted to do it. I wanted to bring him out myself.

(pause)

I hope that's alright.

(pause)

FAYE. It's fine.

(pause)

ETTA. The, uh.

(pause)

It's not settled yet but the service will most likely be this coming Saturday. Short's Funeral Chapel. Late morning.

(pause)

If – any of you would like to come.

(Silence. Then outside, the sound of an approaching car, a car engine shutting off. Everyone looks toward the doors.)

(ETTA *goes to the bed, looking at* **GERALD.)**

(silence)

(The sound of a car door closing.)

(silence)

(Then, for the first time, we hear the sound of the outer glass doors sliding open.)

(A slight pause.)

(The doors slide open. Just as the doors finish opening, the stage goes dark except for a small pool of light surrounding **GERALD** *and* **ETTA.)**

(In the background, we hear the opening of Arvo Pärt's "Für Alina.")

(ETTA *pulls the sheets down from over* **GERALD**'s *head. He opens his eyes.)*

You're listening to it again tonight?

(pause)

You haven't listened to this one in years and now you're listening to it all the time. You used to tell me it was overrated, that objectively speaking it was one of Pärt's least interesting compositions. You remember?

(**ETTA** *starts tucking* **GERALD** *into bed.*)

GERALD. The music, it –.

...

...

I'm not hearing it.

ETTA. We can't turn it up louder, it's past seven, we're not / supposed –

GERALD. No it's there, I'm listening to it, I'm –.

...

...

I'm not hearing it.

(*pause*)

ETTA. There's a storm coming, that's what they're saying. Big one. So I don't want you out wandering around, I want you to stay in bed. Gerald?

(**GERALD** *looks at her.*)

Did you hear what I said?

GERALD. I –

ETTA. There's a big storm coming. So you must *stay here.* Understand?

GERALD. The music, it –.

...

...

There are silences in the music.

(*pause*)

ETTA. Yes, the music has / some –

GERALD. The people without faces, the ones at the end of the bed, the –. They look at me through the silences in the music.

...

Through the whole note rests,
each rest –

the people without faces
staring at me,
staring at –
...
...
...
I can't hear the music.

> (**ETTA** *stares at him.*)

ETTA. Gerald, you –.

> (*pause*)

You know what this is, it's Arvo Pärt, you know this.

GERALD. I can't hear the music.

> (**ETTA** *takes his head gently in her hands, making him look at her.*)

ETTA. *You know this.*

> (*pause*)

It's Arvo Pärt, it's "Für Alina" by Arvo Pärt, you used to / say that –

GERALD. I can't hear it.
...
...
I can't.

> (**ETTA** *stares at him for a moment in silence, then searches around in the sheets for a moment.*)

ETTA. Alright, I think –. I think you should go to sleep, I think we're done with the music for tonight.

> (**ETTA** *finds the remote to the stereo in the sheets, turns off the music.*)

You'll go to sleep and you'll feel better in the morning. You'll feel better after a good night's rest, I promise that you'll –

GERALD. Am I at home?
...

…

Am I home?

> (**ETTA** *stares at him, saying nothing. He stares back at her. Finally, he gives up, looking away. He leans back in bed, staring up.*)

> (*silence*)

GERALD. I'm cold.

> (*silence*)

> (*Finally,* **ETTA** *slowly lifts up the sheets and crawls into bed with him. She wraps her arms around* **GERALD.**)

ETTA. You'll feel better in the morning, just –.

> (*pause*)

Close your eyes.

> (**GERALD** *finally closes his eyes.*)

> (*silence*)

See you in the future.

> (*pause*)

GERALD. I don't – …

…

I don't know what you mean.

…

…

…

I don't know what you mean.

> (*pause*)

ETTA. See you in the future.

> (*They continue to hold one another.*)

End of Play